Text copyright © 2007
by Harriet Ziefert
Illustrations copyright © 2007
by Emily Bolam
All rights reserved / CIP Data is available.
Published in the United States 2007 by
Blue Apple Books
P.O. Box 1380, Maplewood, N.J. 07040
www.blueapplebooks.com

Distributed in the U.S. by Chronicle Books
First Edition
Printed in China

ISBN 13: 978-1-59354-603-8
ISBN 10: 1-59354-603-3

1 3 5 7 9 10 8 6 4 2

BUZZY's BALLOON

BY **HARRIET ZIEFERT**

PICTURES BY
EMILY BOLAM

Blue Apple Books

Red shoes, yellow shoes,
green shoes, blues.
Which do you think
Buzzy will choose?

Buzzy picks blue.
What about *you*?

Balloons in reds.
Balloons in blues.

Which do you think
Buzzy will choose?

Buzzy picks blue.
What about *you*?

Balloon on a string
tied to his bed—

Buzzy likes it
near his head.

Morning comes,
the air's all out.

Buzzy gives
a worried shout.

"Mommy, Mommy,
Balloon's no more.

Make it like
it was before!"

Mommy knows
just what to do.

"I'll blow it up
again for you."

Mommy blows,
and blows,
and blows.

The balloon
grows . . .

and grows . . .

and **grows!**

Mommy says,
"It's good as new.
I blew it up again for you."

Balloon on a string,

balloon on a string!

Mommies are a
wonderful thing!

"My balloon
is blue . . .

My balloon's
up high . . .

Look at how
my balloon
can fly!"

Catch it,

chase it,
throw it,
shove it.

Hold it,
hug it,

squish it,

love it.

MOMMY. . .

MOMMY!

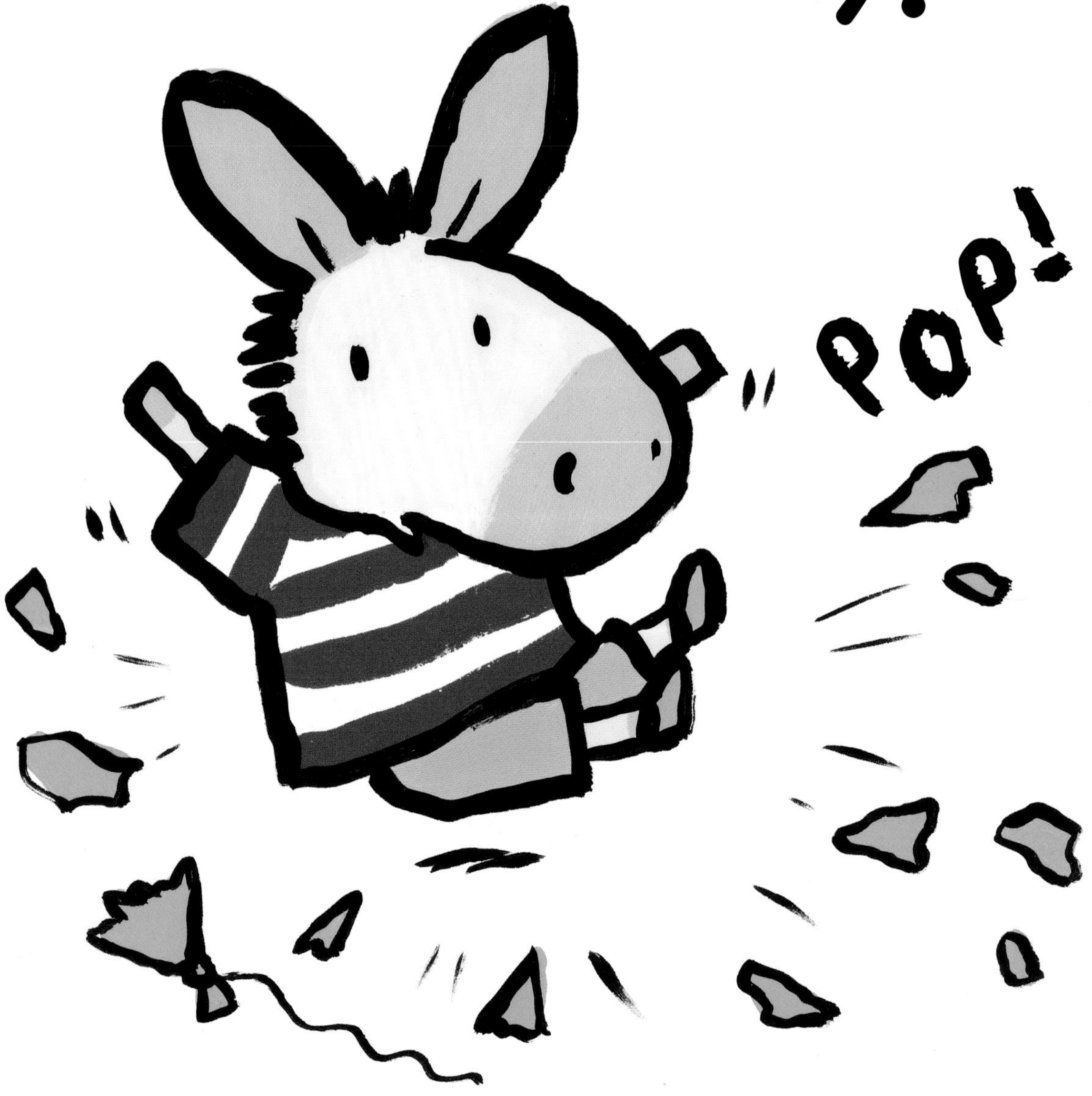

"I can't fix the balloon for you.
Once it's popped,
a balloon is through.

Find another toy and play.
A popped balloon shouldn't
ruin your day."

Buzzy doesn't want to play.
No, no, no—not right away.
Not with a puzzle. Not with a ball.
Not with anything at all!

Then he sees a good old friend—
and his feelings start to mend.

"Okay, Lamb, I'll play with you.
You won't burst like a balloon will do."

THE END